Fr Phineas!

Birds I've met through the Alphabet

Written by
Amy Tietjen

by

...Fitts

Vabella Publishing
P.O. Box 1052
Carrollton, Georgia 30112
www.vabella.com

Manufactured in the United States of America

13-digit ISBN 978-1-938230-33-2

Library of Congress Control Number 2013905957

10 9 8 7 6 5 4 3 2 1

For my family, an exceptional flock of rare and exotic birds.

~A.J.T.

To all my 'peeps.' I thank you all for the encouragement and support.

~S.F.

Adelaide ate apples
until she looked like one.

Bernie was a busy bird
in rain, and snow, and sun.

Cory came and went so fast
he almost looked see-through.

Drew said climbing tree trunks
was his favorite thing to do.

Emma sang and danced all day
as if she were a star.

Floyd sat in the tops of trees
and searched for food afar.

Griffin hunted just like Floyd
but did so in the day.

Hunter and his feathered friends,
well, all they did was play.

Inga liked to eat a lot,
so she would visit feeders.

Joseph was a smarty-pants;
he hung out with readers.

Kelsey was artistic,
thus her nest was multi-colored.

Laura was so patient
she could tolerate a dullard.

Markus had a messy beak
from eating lots of berries.

Nora had a love of lore -
she always looked for fairies.

Oliver liked mystery,
thus he was always cloaked.

Piper was a sooty bird—
her friends all thought she smoked.

Quixote liked a quiet life,
his favorite word was "shush."

Renee was a little shy,
so she hid in a bush.

Sydney welcomed everyone
by offering them her wing.

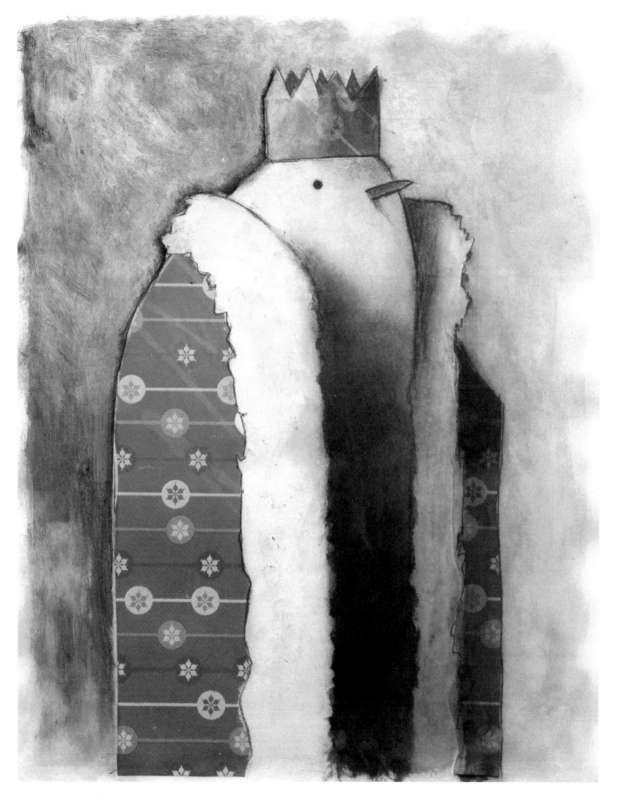

Tim had the reputation
of dressing like a king.

Uma chose a funny way
to get from place to place.

Verna looked a little strange,
for she was mostly face.

William was a blue-ish bird,
though he was rarely sad.

Xavier's best friend was a frog,
so he stayed at his pad.

Yenna was a taller bird—
her legs were very long.

Zach was sure that all the birds should sing their own sweet song.

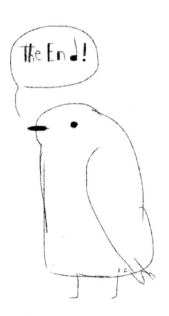